# HAMSTER PRINCESS
## Little Red Rodent Hood

# HAMSTER PRINCESS
## Little Red Rodent Hood

by
### URSULA VERNON

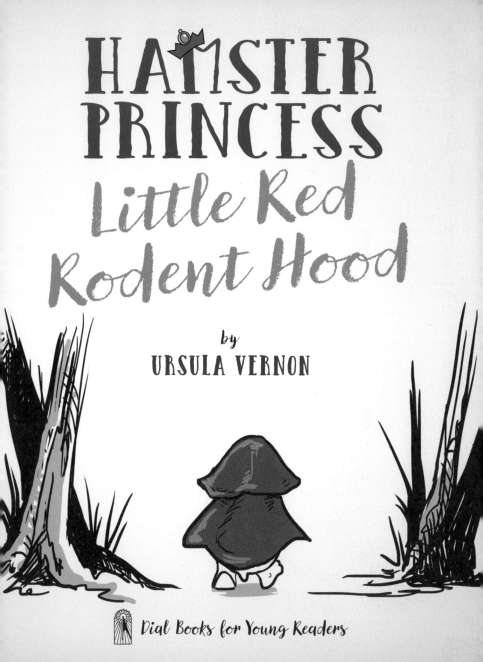

Dial Books for Young Readers

DIAL BOOKS FOR YOUNG READERS
PENGUIN YOUNG READERS GROUP
An imprint of Penguin Random House LLC
375 Hudson Street
New York, NY 10014

Library of Congress Cataloging-in-Publication Data
Names: Vernon, Ursula, author, illustrator. | Title: Little Red Rodent Hood / Ursula Vernon.
Description: New York, NY : Dial Books for Young Readers, [2018] | Series: Hamster princess ; 6 | Summary: A little girl in a red cape asks for Princess Harriet Hamsterbone's help with a pack of weasel-wolves who want to eat her grandmother, but after meeting everyone, Harriet is not sure who to trust.
Identifiers: LCCN 2018009478 | ISBN 9780399186585 (hardback) | ISBN 9780399186608 (ebook)
Subjects: | CYAC: Princesses—Fiction. | Adventure and adventurers—Fiction. | Hypnotism—Fiction. | Kidnapping—Fiction. | Hamsters—Fiction. | Humorous stories. | BISAC: JUVENILE FICTION / Fairy Tales & Folklore / Adaptations. | JUVENILE FICTION / Animals / Mice, Hamsters, Guinea Pigs, etc.. | JUVENILE FICTION / Humorous Stories. | Classification: LCC PZ7.V5985 Lit 2018 | DDC [Fic]—dc23
LC record available at https://lccn.loc.gov/2018009478

Printed in China
10  9  8  7  6  5  4  3  2  1

Design by Jennifer Kelly
Text set in Minister Std Light

For all the little girls
who grew up wanting
to be werewolves.

# HAMSTER PRINCESS
## Little Red Rodent Hood

# CHAPTER 1

Princess Harriet? Princess Harriet?"

Harriet Hamsterbone—princess, warrior, breaker of curses, and recreational cliff-diver—looked up from where she was practicing her sword work on a dummy. "Eh? What?"

She was working in the courtyard of her father's castle. A small hamster stood in the entryway, wearing a red cloak. The hood was drawn down, but even so, Harriet could see that she was very young.

"Princess Harriet?" The little girl had a high, lisping voice, of the sort that adults thought was adorable and precious and that made other kids immediately suspicious.

Harriet stopped and wiped the sweat from her fur. "Can I help you?"

"I'm looking for . . ." The girl trailed off. "Err . . . why are you hitting that dummy with a sword?"

GOTTA PRACTICE MY SWORD WORK.

"In case you're attacked by dummies?" asked the girl.

"Because the dummy's the only one that will hold still," said Harriet's best friend, Wilbur, who was reading a book on the sidelines. He looked up. "When she comes after *me* with a sword, I scream and run away."

"Then you must be Princess Harriet," said the girl with relief. "Thank goodness! You're supposed to be the best, nicest, kindest, sweetest, most wonderful princess in the whole world!"

". . . uh," said Harriet. She would have accepted "fiercest" or "bravest," but "kindest" and "sweetest" were definitely stretching things.

"I have a terrible problem!" the little girl said. "They're after my grandmother!"

Wilbur and Harriet looked at her blankly.

"You have to save her! She's all I've got!"

"Who's 'they'?" asked Wilbur.

"Where's your grandmother?" asked Harriet.

The little girl sighed. "It's complicated."

"Start at the beginning," suggested Wilbur.

"Or start at the point where you need me to hit something with a sword," said Harriet. Harriet had what her old teachers would call "a straightforward personality with clearly defined goals."

YES! THEM!
THE STINKY AWFUL
WOLVES!

"We just moved here, but there's a huge horrible one in the woods! The biggest one I've ever seen! And a bunch of others too. They're lurking around my grandmother's cottage!"

"They're lurkers, all right," said Harriet, narrowing her eyes. "And you say there are a lot?"

"Packs and packs. But there's a big one in charge! Huge! Awful! Smelly!"

Harriet's mind filled with visions of a coming invasion. "A horde of weasel-wolves?"

NO PROBLEM!
I DON'T CARE HOW
MANY THERE ARE!
LET ME AT 'EM!

"Err . . ." said Wilbur. "Are you sure maybe you and your grandmother shouldn't move out of the cottage? If there are so many?"

"Grandmother can't leave the cottage," said the little girl primly. "She's not well. I take care of her."

"So you walked here all by yourself?" said Wilbur, astonished. "Past all the weasel-wolves?"

"Yes?" said the little girl.

"You're awfully young to be alone in the woods," said Wilbur, which was true, but not the sort of thing that it would occur to Harriet to say.

"They're only really dangerous at night," said the girl. "I need to get back before it's dark, though. In fact, I should leave now."

"We'll go with you," said Harriet. "Give me five minutes to clean up and get my good sword."

The little girl in red tapped her foot impatiently the whole time. Harriet and Wilbur saddled up their riding quail and followed her down the road.

"Qwerk!" said Mumfrey, Harriet's riding quail, who didn't like weasel-wolves at all.

"Qwerr-rr-rrk," said Hyacinth, Wilbur's riding quail, who liked weasel-wolves even less than Mumfrey did.

"Oh, what beautiful quail!" said the little girl, flinging her arms around Hyacinth's neck. "Aren't they just the bestest, most wonderful quail in the whole world?"

"Qwerk?" said Hyacinth, which was Quail for "Err, I guess?"

Mumfrey looked suspiciously at the little girl. "Qwerk," he said, not quite under his breath.

"Problem?" said Harriet.

". . . Qwerk . . ." said Mumfrey, which was Quail for "No . . . I guess that's something a normal person would say . . . maybe . . ."

Harriet followed his gaze to the little girl. She came up to the middle of Harriet's chest and her cloak was blazing scarlet, the color of poppies. It wasn't the sort of thing you'd wear in the woods if you were trying to be sneaky. People could probably see that cloak from the next kingdom.

Still, she needed help. Harriet was the princess, so it was her job to take care of the people in her kingdom, and that meant finding out why the weasel-wolves were harassing innocent grandmothers in the woods.

They passed the tiny village of Lonesquash and looked down the road toward the forest. The countryside was tranquil, with broad farm fields and narrow bands of shaded woodland. Grain waved gently in the fields, almost up to the edge of the woods. It did not look like the sort of place where you expected to find a gathering army of weasel-wolves.

Still, Harriet knew that danger could lurk in the most unexpected places. You always had to be on your guard.

"So you live out here?" asked Wilbur.

"Oh, no," said Red. "I wish we did. It's so pretty and nice! But we live in the woods. Which are also pretty and nice, I guess. If you like trees." She looked briefly doubtful. "Which I do."

"Trees are nice," offered Wilbur.

"Yes! And these are the bestest, nicest, most wonderful trees in the whole wide world!"

"And you live there with your grandmother?"

"Yes! She's the bestest, nicest, kindest grand-mother—"

"In the whole wide world?" finished Harriet.

"Yes! How did you know?"

"Lucky guess," said Harriet. She spurred Mum-frey and they trotted down the road and into the forest.

# CHAPTER 2

The weasel-wolves were not hard to find.

Actually, they were pretty hard to miss. The road to the cottage had trees on both sides, and lurking behind each tree was a weasel-wolf.

Harriet put her hand on her sword and narrowed her eyes.

It was odd, though. They didn't actually *look* dangerous. There were no glaring eyes or gleaming fangs, and nobody seemed to be obviously slavering for hamster meat.

Instead, they looked worried.

"It's weird," said Wilbur as they kept riding. "They don't look like they're about to attack."

"Qweerrrkkkk..." muttered Hyacinth. She kept trying to inch away from the trees, which didn't work very well because then she was closer to the trees on the other side of the road.

"They're weasel-wolves," said Harriet. "They're *always* about to attack. I once walked through the middle of a pack while they were sleeping and they attacked *in their sleep*."

The little girl tromping down the path ahead of them didn't seem frightened. Red glared at the wolves as if they had personally offended her.

Harriet slowed the quail and looked around.

The weasel-wolves in the woods all immediately attempted to look like bushes or trees or bits of moss. They weren't very good at it.

"Hurry up!" called Red. "For the best princess in the whole wide world, you're really slow!"

"Look," said Harriet, annoyed, "something really weird is going on here and we're all trying to pretend like it's not, which is stupid. Why aren't they attacking?"

I'M NOT SCARED OF STUPID STINKY WEASEL-WOLVES!

"Then why did you come and ask for help?" asked Harriet, baffled.

"You should be scared!" added Wilbur, who was having a hard time staying in the saddle, as Hyacinth wobbled from one side of the path to the other. "Weasel-wolves are scary!"

"These aren't," said Red, over her shoulder. "*These* are just normal weasel-wolves. Some of them are even sort of cute. It's the big one you have to worry about!"

THE BIG ONE?

"The leader," said Red darkly. "When he shows up, then it'll be dangerous. He's the worst and meanest and stinkiest! And he only comes out at night!"

"Qwerrrrk . . ." said Mumfrey, which was Quail for "I don't like the sound of this . . ."

Harriet frowned.

She looked over at the weasel-wolves in the trees. The weasel-wolves had bunched up into a large group. She had to admit, they still didn't look hostile, though. They looked like small children who had lost their parents somewhere in a crowd and didn't know where to go next.

Harriet wasn't used to weasel-wolves that didn't attack. It made her wonder what on earth was going on.

"I liked it better when they tried to eat me," she said to Wilbur. "Then I waved my sword around and they waved their claws around, and everybody knew where they stood."

"Errr . . ." Wilbur wasn't sure what to say about that. He rather liked not being attacked, but the weasel-wolves were certainly acting strange.

Harriet scowled, then came to a decision. "Hold up, Red!" she called. "I want to see what's going on with these weasel-wolves."

WE DON'T HAVE TIME!

"Maybe you should go on ahead," said Wilbur. "Except—err—well, no, they might attack, so maybe don't—" He floundered. Obviously the little girl had already walked through the gathered weasel-wolves, so she couldn't be in that much danger, could she?

Harriet had no such concerns. "Run along to your grandmother's house, then," she said, drawing her sword. "We'll meet you there when we can."

"Ugh!" said Red. Then she cleared her throat. "I mean, okay, Princess! But please come quickly, before they eat my grandmother!"

She hurried away.

"Look out!" said Wilbur. "There's two weasel-wolves . . . in front . . . of you . . ."

He trailed off. Red was walking right up to them, without a trace of fear.

Harriet started forward, sword at the ready.

The little girl stared at the weasel-wolves.

She was tiny compared to them and all she did was stare, but both the weasels inched backward.

Harriet couldn't blame them. There was something disturbingly intense about that stare. Red
looked as if she were glaring into their very souls.

They slunk into the woods, making small, whim-
pering noises.

Red made a sound like "Hmmf!" and stomped
down the road.

As soon as Red had vanished, a sigh went
through the weasel-wolves. It sounded almost
like . . . relief?

Hyacinth the quail was in no mood to feel relieved. She qwerked and bounced up and down on her toes anxiously, ready to run.

"Err . . . Harriet?" said Wilbur. "Is this a good idea?"

"There is something very weird going on here!" hissed Harriet. "That is a very strange little girl!"

Wilbur frowned. "I thought she was very sweet."

"You would."

"What's that supposed to—no." Wilbur held up a hand. "Let's not do this while we're surrounded by predators!"

"That's the other weird bit! The weasel-wolves! They aren't supposed to be scared of little girls staring at them! They *attack* people."

"Sometimes, yeah. I mean, so do you, though."

"Hey! I only attack bad people!"

Wilbur waited.

"Fine, fine, one time it was some actors, but it was a really realistic dragon costume and I didn't realize it was actually four rats in a suit. And I did apologize. And Dad paid for the repairs to the papier-mâché."

"I don't think these are weasel costumes. But—hsst! What are they doing?"

The weasel-wolves had begun to move. One by one, they pulled back, leaving a broad corridor down the middle of the pack.

Down that corridor came the biggest weasel-wolf that Harriet had ever seen.

# CHAPTER 3

He was huge, bigger than Harriet, and dark gray, the color of storm clouds. He had a black mask, like most weasel-wolves, but also black paws and a black tail.

The gray weasel-wolf moved toward them, eyes fixed on the hamsters.

"Right," said Harriet, holding up her sword. "That's far enough."

He stopped.

They stared at each other for a moment that

seemed to stretch out further and further. Hyacinth shifted her feet nervously. Mumfrey flicked his curved topknot back and forth.

"The big one," said Wilbur. "Red said he only came out at night!"

Harriet didn't want to take her eyes off the weasel-wolf, but she could see by the shadows that it was still only late afternoon. "Does *he* know that?"

The big weasel-wolf sat up on his hind legs and

said something that sounded like "growrr-groww-wfff-grlllf!"

"Okay," said Harriet. "Uh." She looked at Wilbur. Wilbur shrugged helplessly. He didn't speak Weasel-wolf any more than she did.

"Grrawwlf!"

"What do you think he's saying?" whispered Wilbur.

"How should I know? I left my Weasel-wolf dictionary at home!"

The big gray weasel-wolf in front sighed, then turned and barked at the ones behind him.

There was a stir in the ranks, and two weasel-wolves slunk forward. One was holding a . . . a . . .

"Is that a sheet of paper?" whispered Wilbur.

"And a crayon? Where did weasel-wolves get *crayons?*"

"Maybe they ate someone with a crayon," said Harriet darkly.

The weasel-wolves set them down in front of the big gray one, who nodded. He glanced up at Harriet, then back down at the paper. Then he picked the crayon up in his mouth and began to draw.

Harriet was impressed despite herself. Drawing

with a crayon in your mouth had to be nearly impossible. Nevertheless, the gray weasel-wolf finished in a few moments, then sat back.

One of his—henchweasels? Harriet didn't know what to call them—picked up the paper. Unlike the others, this one was so small that Harriet could have lifted it up with one hand. It was barely half the size of Wilbur, and not even Hyacinth could find it scary.

It carried the paper forward, slinking lower and lower, until it was practically flat on the ground.

"It's fine," said Harriet, realizing that the weasel-wolf was scared of her. "You can bring me the note."

The tiny weasel-wolf dropped it at Harriet's feet. It bobbed its head in a quick little bow, then darted back to the safety of the pack.

Harriet picked it up cautiously.

"Aww," said Wilbur. "Look, they even drew little stink-lines."

"I don't stink! Except when I'm covered in ichor."

"Ichor?" asked Wilbur.

"The goo that comes out of giant spiders," said Harriet. "Or out of any giant insects, slimes, and other assorted monsters, really."

BASICALLY, IF YOU HIT IT WITH A SWORD AND IT DOESN'T BLEED, BUT SOMETHING NASTY AND GREEN COMES OUT, *THAT'S* ICHOR.

Wilbur did not look as if this addition to his vocabulary had made him any happier.

"About the weasel-wolves . . ." he said.

"No, they're mammals, so they have regular blood," said Harriet, who had a very one-track mind. "No ichor there at all."

"About the note!"

"Oh. Right." Harriet examined the note again. "He's . . . he's asking for help?"

The big weasel-wolf nodded vigorously at her.

"But why would you need my help?"

The weasel-wolf sat up on his hind legs and attempted to do some sort of mime. Harriet and Wilbur stared at him, trying to figure out what he could be saying.

THERE'S . . . SOMETHING WITH . . . TEETH? CLAWS?

"It's always evil clowns!" said Harriet.

"It has never once been evil clowns," said Wilbur grimly.

"That's because they're sneaky."

After nearly a minute, they had determined that it was not, in fact, evil clowns, but they were no closer to figuring out what the problem actually was.

"Sorry," said Wilbur. "I don't think we understand what help you need."

Harriet suddenly realized that she was talking to an enormous weasel-wolf. "And wait. Why would we help you? You're a weasel-wolf! You eat people!"

The tiny, sad weasel-wolf gave her a pitiful look. Harriet immediately felt like a monster.

The big weasel-wolf shook his head, looking disgusted. One by one, the weasel-wolves melted away into the forest, until Wilbur and Harriet stood alone on the path with their quail.

# CHAPTER 4

I have no idea what's going on," said Harriet. "I mean, usually that doesn't bother me, but I have even less idea than usual now."

"So now the weasel-wolves want help?" said Wilbur. "And Red wants help with the weasel-wolves? Does everybody in this whole forest need help? And was that big one the one she was talking about?"

"Those are excellent questions, Wilbur," said Harriet. "I have no answers for any of them."

They began walking down the road in what was presumably the direction of Red's grandmother's house.

"They could be cleverly drawing me out," said Harriet. "By writing a note. Then they'll attack when I ride to the rescue!"

"I'm not saying you're wrong," said Wilbur, in the tone of voice he used to indicate that Harriet was almost certainly wrong, "but why wouldn't they have attacked as soon as you showed up? What are the odds that weasel-wolves are that smart?"

"They wrote a note. That's pretty smart."

"Yeah, but their spelling was awful."

"Just because you can't spell doesn't mean you can't lay a clever trap, Wilbur! Very few diabolical traps are dependent on your ability to spell a word like—err—"

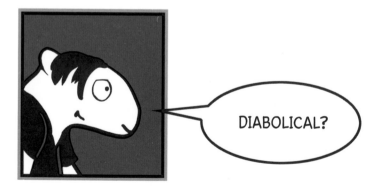

FOR EXAMPLE.

"Qwerk-qwerk-qwerk-qwerk . . ." began Mum-frey, which was Quail for "D-I-A-B . . ." But then he couldn't remember if the next letter was a *Qwerk* or a *Qwerk* and trailed off into silence.

"I just think that if they were trying to lure you into a trap, they probably wouldn't have included the stink lines," said Wilbur.

Harriet grumbled under her breath. The idea that weasel-wolves might need her help was not sitting well with her.

"Well, let's see what Red wants us to do. Maybe then everything will make sense."

The shadows lengthened as they went down the road. Occasionally Harriet heard a twig snap or leaves rustle, as if a weasel-wolf was watching them, but when she looked back, no one was there.

It took longer than Harriet expected to reach Red's grandmother's cottage. The road snaked back and forth through the woods, and she had the feeling that they were walking a long time without making much progress. It would have been much quicker simply to cut through the woods, but then they'd risk losing the path altogether. They might even wind up at a completely different cottage and confuse the inhabitants as to why there was a princess banging on their door after dark.

People in Harriet's kingdom had developed a certain paranoia about having a princess show up at the door in the middle of the night. It usually meant that something was invading and no one was going to get a decent night's sleep.

The sun had just dropped below the trees when the road opened up into a clearing and they came at last to Grandmother's house.

# CHAPTER 5

In the center of the clearing was a cottage. It was a tiny cottage with a metal roof and a chimney and even a window box full of flowers. Smoke puffed from the chimney and the smell of fresh-baked bread filled the clearing.

The cottage was up on wheels like a wagon. Everything about it was scaled down. The door was smaller, the windows were smaller. Everything was small and neat and compact.

Harriet had met travelers who lived in wagons, usually pulled by quail or even draft chickens. She couldn't see any sign of animals to pull the wheeled cottage, though.

It would have been a picturesque scene, except for one thing.

Next to the cottage, also on wheels, stood a massive iron cage.

". . . uh," said Wilbur.

"That's . . . um . . . different . . ." said Harriet. "Not a lot of picturesque cottages with big wheeled cages outside."

"Perhaps they have a very odd sense of decor?" said Wilbur.

"Yeah . . ." said Harriet. "What would that even be? Giant Cage Chic?"

"Qwerrrrk . . ." said Mumfrey, which was Quail for "I don't know what to think."

Red stood on the steps of the cottage. When she saw Harriet and Wilbur arrive, she clasped her hands together. "You made it! I was so worried when you took so long, even though you're the best princess in the whole—"

"Sorry," said Harriet, who wasn't particularly sorry. "There were weasel-wolves."

"Did you beat them up?"

"No . . ." Harriet began.

Red's worshipful expression slipped for a moment. "What?"

WHAT KIND OF WARRIOR ARE YOU!?

"One who doesn't attack things that haven't attacked me first!" Harriet yelled back, which was more or less true, although she had sometimes made exceptions for things that were a whole lot bigger than she was.

Red stamped her foot. Harriet raised her eyebrows. "Okay, see, I don't approve of that," she said. "You should never stomp your foot. People don't take you seriously if you do that."

"I'm taking her seriously . . ." said Wilbur, not quite under his breath.

"Yes, but you take *everything* seriously."

The little girl folded her arms. "You can't come in now," she said. "I'm sorry. I know Grandmother would want to meet you because she's the best grandmother in the world and you're a princess. But you were too slow! Grandmother's asleep."

Harriet paused.

She tried very hard not to be treated special just because she was a princess. Being a princess wasn't her fault. She'd been born into royalty and she knew that people treated princesses differently from peasants. It was her job to use that fact for good, not evil.

Nevertheless, she wasn't used to people going to sleep instead of meeting with her. People usually stayed awake to meet princesses. Particularly when they'd asked for her help.

"Uh," said Harriet. "Is she . . . uh . . . well, okay. Should we come back tomorrow?"

Strangely, the little girl looked up at the sky before answering. Harriet followed her gaze but couldn't see anything except dark blue sky. The first stars were starting to come out and the moon was washing cold blue light over the ground.

"Don't trust anything the big one says?" Harriet said, baffled. "But you said it's a weasel-wolf. They don't . . ."

"... talk," finished Harriet, blinking at the door. Red had dashed inside and slammed it behind her. She looked at Wilbur. Wilbur looked at her.

"Do we go bang on the door?" she asked uncertainly. Monsters she understood. Very small girls throwing tantrums were a little outside of her league. (Harriet was an only child because her mother said that her nerves could only take so much.)

"I don't think we want to wake up an old lady," said Wilbur. "I mean, when my grandmother was alive, and she went to sleep for the night, you didn't wake her up unless the house was on fire."

Harriet nodded. "I guess we could go home and come back in the morning?"

Wilbur looked back through the woods. "We could try, but . . . uh . . ."

He pointed.

After dark, most quail had the urge to tuck their heads under their wings and roost. Hyacinth already had her head under her wing. Mumfrey was doing better, but he was definitely flagging.

"No time for that, Mumfrey! We've got work to do!"

"Qwerrgkk . . ." muttered Mumfrey, which was Quail for "It's not my fault, yawns just happen."

Harriet sighed. "I guess we're gonna have to camp in the woods tonight, then."

"With all the weasel-wolves?" said Wilbur.

"Yeah. And according to Red, we're not sup-posed to trust anything they say."

Wilbur looked very confused. "Do you think that's going to be an issue?"

"I tell you," said Harriet thoughtfully, leading Mumfrey toward the woods, "I'm starting to wonder . . ."

# CHAPTER 6

They found a small clearing in the woods where a tree had fallen and left a gap in the leafy canopy. They could look up and see the sky turn from deep blue to velvet black.

One by one, more stars came out.

Two by two, the eyes of weasel-wolves began to shine in the dark woods.

"Okay," said Wilbur. "Now *that* is creepy."

"Qwerrrkkk . . ." said Hyacinth, which was Quail for "I don't like this! This is bad!" Then she yawned.

"Qwerk!" said Mumfrey, which was Quail for "I'll protect you, but yeah, this is bad." Then he yawned too, because yawns are as contagious for quail as for everyone else.

"I'd *love* it if my eyes glowed at night," said Harriet.

"That would be *incredibly* creepy," said Wilbur.

"Yeah, wouldn't it be cool?"

THINK ABOUT IT! YOU COULD LURK AND YOUR ENEMIES WOULD JUST SEE EYES! CAN YOU IMAGINE HOW UNSETTLING THAT WOULD BE?

"I don't have to imagine it," said Wilbur testily, "the weasel-wolves are *right there!*"

"Oh, uh . . . right."

The moon came out from behind a cloud, throwing light across the trees. It made all the shadows sharp-edged and turned everything silvery-blue.

There were really quite a lot of weasel-wolves.

"They didn't attack before," said Harriet. "Maybe they have another note."

"You're alive," said a voice behind them.

Harriet jumped and came down with her sword

raised, standing between the voice and Wilbur and the quail.

"Qwerrrk!" cried Hyacinth, which was Quail for "I am terrified and also very sleepy!"

At first, all Harriet could see was another pair of glowing eyes. They appeared far back in the woods, larger than the others, and began to approach.

"It's all right," called the voice. "I'm not going to hurt you."

THAT'S RIGHT, YOU'RE NOT.

She lifted her sword warily, not threatening, but definitely keeping the blade between herself and those eyes. Just because the voice seemed—not *friendly,* maybe, but not hostile—didn't mean that this wasn't all an incredibly elaborate trap.

The eyes were higher off the ground than any weasel-wolf Harriet had ever seen. The owner had to be taller than she was. This was unsettling, but Harriet had fought giants before. It just meant that she punched *up.*

"It's got to be the big one!" hissed Wilbur in her ear.

"Thank you, Wilbur, I had figured that out!"

The big gray weasel-wolf stepped forward into the circle of moonlight. Except that he wasn't a weasel-wolf any longer. He was large and shaggy and standing upright.

In fact, he looked like . . . a hamster?

The hamster/weasel-wolf/who-knew-what-else smiled. He had very sharp teeth.

"Nice to meet you, Princess Harriet," he said. "My name is Grey."

# CHAPTER 7

**Y**ou're a were-weasel!" said Wilbur.

"No, I'm not," said the large gray hamster. "I am a were-*hamster*. I was born a weasel-wolf, but I was bitten by a hamster under the full moon, and now I turn into one for three days a month."

Wilbur and Harriet both stared at him. "That can happen?" asked Harriet.

"Indeed it can."

"But who's the hamster who bit you?" asked Wilbur.

"Funny story . . ." The former weasel-wolf pointed at Harriet.

OH. HUH. REALLY?

Wilbur stared first at him, then at Harriet. "Harriet? You *bit* this guy?"

"It's certainly possible."

"You don't *remember?!*"

"Hey, I bite a lot of people," said Harriet. "Once you've dropped your sword, you use whatever you've got."

"You said you didn't eat people!"

"Biting is not eating," said Harriet with dignity.

"And how would that even work?" Wilbur clutched his head. "How could Harriet turn you into a were-hamster when she's not a were-hamster?"

"I might be," said Harriet. "I have hidden depths. Have we ever hung out together during the full moon?"

"Yes, we have," said Wilbur. "And furthermore, I *know* you're not, because if you were, you'd tell *everybody.* You'd be all *Hey guys, check this out! I can turn into a weasel!*"

. . . OKAY, THAT'S FAIR.

Grey grinned. "It's the Changes," he said, as if he were explaining something obvious.

"The what, now?"

"The Changes. Harriet was in the wrong place at the right time. If I'd gotten bitten that night by . . . by a quail, say, I'd probably grow feathers on the full moon."

"Qwerk," said Mumfrey, which was Quail for "Would that be so bad?"

Wilbur looked baffled.

Grey sighed. "Look, have you heard of were-weasel-wolves?"

"Of course, but I didn't know they really existed!"

Harriet and Grey exchanged glances. "Well, yeah, obviously," said Harriet. "I mean, why wouldn't they?"

"But I thought those were just legends!"

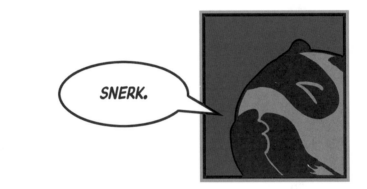

"I just never met one before."

"Right," said Grey. "So everybody's heard of were-weasel-wolves. We're famous for it. We bite you, you turn into one of us, right?"

"I'm with you so far," said Wilbur.

"Well, the only reason that we can do that is because we're . . . um . . . inherently changey ourselves. The technical term is 'metamorphic instability,' at least according to a wizard I ate once."

Wilbur put his hand over his eyes. "You *ate* him."

"Look, he wasn't a nice wizard."

"Don't get distracted with irrelevancies, Wilbur!" said Harriet.

Grey waited politely for them to stop yelling at each other. "Okay," he said. "So basically weasel-wolves come down with the Changes the way you come down with lizard pox, right? You get it once as a kid and never get it again?"

"I remember," said Harriet grimly. "I itched for *days*. Mom made me wear socks on my hands so I wouldn't scratch."

"Well, I had the Changes. And if nothing had bitten me, I'd be a regular weasel-wolf, but then you came along, and I was hungry and Harriet . . . well . . . y'know."

AREN'T YOU GOING TO APOLOGIZE?

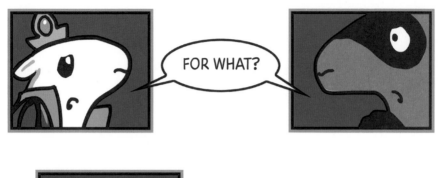

"Uh . . ." Harriet rubbed the back of her neck. "Is that a thing I should apologize for? I mean, I'm sure I had a good reason to bite him . . ."

"Oh, definitely. I was trying to kill and eat you," said Grey. "These things happen."

"I still don't remember it, sorry," said Harriet. "I mean, a lot of people try to kill and eat me. It's sort of an occupational hazard."

"Well, it was a few years ago. You were in our woods. And once you bit me, some of my pack-mates jumped you and I managed to limp away, so no one died."

"There, you see?" said Harriet. She was glad that Grey understood these things.

Wilbur stared at them as if they were both nuts.

"No hard feelings," said Grey.

WAIT . . .
HE TRIED TO KILL
YOU AND YOU BIT HIM
AND TURNED HIM INTO A
WERE-HAMSTER, AND
YOU'RE BOTH OKAY
WITH THIS?!

"I'm not making it weird!" yelled Wilbur. "It's already weird! *You two are weird!*"

"I'm a weasel-wolf," said Grey. "Biting happens. It's not worth getting worked up about."

"There, you see?" said Harriet. "Perfectly reasonable."

She studied Grey thoughtfully. If you saw him on the street, as a hamster, you'd still notice something strange about him. His teeth were sharper than a regular hamster's and his eyes had the same eerie glow as the weasel-wolves.

"I mean, I'd rather not turn into a hamster on the full moon, but there are worse things," said Grey. "Like if somebody's got silver weapons."

"What's wrong with silver?" asked Wilbur.

"I'm a were-hamster," said Grey. "I have a very bad allergy to silver."

"Like hay fever?"

"Like it causes me to die."

UH . . .

"Yeah," said Grey. "Were-hamsters call silver *moon-drinker metal*. It's like it pulls the moonlight right out of you. I fall down in a faint."

"That's not so bad . . ."

"Also it burns. Like acid."

". . . not great," said Wilbur.

"I don't mind being a were-hamster otherwise," said Grey. "I mean, I can't really *be* killed except with silver."

"Ooh, neat!" said Harriet. "I was invincible once. I kinda miss that." She considered. "I don't suppose I could get you to bite me?"

"Harriet!" said Wilbur, horrified.

"What?"

"You can't get turned into a were-weasel!"

"I'm pretty sure I can, if we time it right. It's the full moon now, so one good chomp ought to—"

"What would your parents say!?" said Wilbur, waving his arms in the air.

Wilbur put his head in his hands.

"Honestly, I'm not seeing a downside to being a were-weasel," said Harriet. "I'd have an amazing bite!"

"We really, really gotta have a talk about all this biting," said Wilbur.

"Oh c'mon, Wilbur. If I were a were-weasel, I wouldn't bite random strangers."

I MEAN, UNLESS THEY *DESERVED* IT . . .

"It's that bit that worries me," said Wilbur, sighing. "Can you wait just a bit? Until we deal with this?"

"Fiiiine . . ." said Harriet, as if not turning into a monster on the full moon was a serious imposition. She turned back to Grey. "Now, why did you send me a note?"

Grey groaned and rubbed his paw over his face. "It's complicated," he said. "But my pack needs help."

"Yeah, I got that," said Harriet. "But why *me*, specifically?"

The were-weasel raised his eyebrows. "Isn't it obvious?"

# CHAPTER 8

Flattery will get you nowhere," said Harriet, although she was secretly rather pleased. "But why do you need help?"

Grey shook his head. "Maybe we should sit down for a few minutes. It's a long story."

Harriet sheathed her sword. If this was a trap, it was a bizarrely convoluted one. The quail had mostly lost their fear of Grey, but they still eyed the weasel-wolf pack in the woods warily.

"I wouldn't have sent a note at all," said Grey,

sitting on a fallen log. "I'd have waited until moon-rise and talked to you like this."

BUT WHEN I SAW THAT THE STRANGE LITTLE GIRL WAS TAKING YOU TO HER COTTAGE, I HAD NO CHOICE.

Harriet suddenly remembered how Red had said not to trust anything the big one said. She must have meant Grey.

This was a problem, because Harriet already liked Grey much more than she had liked Red.

She reminded herself that while Grey was quite a likable weasel-wolf, he was also a weasel-wolf, and thus a vicious predator who ate people. (The fact that he had tried to eat *her* once didn't bother her. In Harriet's world, trying to kill and eat people was practically like a hearty handshake.)

She reminded herself that were-weasels were notoriously dangerous and bloodthirsty.

She reminded herself that Red had come to her for help.

But there was no getting around the fact that neither she nor Mumfrey had liked Red. Harriet might question her own judge of character, but Mumfrey's was extremely sound.

"Why didn't you want me to go in that house?" she said. "And why did you say 'You're alive!' like it was a surprise?"

"Maybe I should start at the beginning," said Grey.

"That would be best," said Wilbur gratefully.

"It all began a few months ago," said Grey. "We started hearing rumors about packs farther east vanishing."

"Vanishing?" said Wilbur.

COMPLETELY GONE. ONE MONTH YOU'D HEAR THEM IN THE HOWL, THE NEXT MONTH THEY'D BE GONE.

"The Howl?" asked Harriet.

"Oh. Yes. The packs all howl on the first day of the new moon. The moon vanishes once a month, you know, during the dark of the moon, and when it comes back, we all howl to greet it."

He rubbed his nose. "We can all hear the packs next to us howling, so we know that they're okay. Except that one Howl, a pack wasn't there anymore. And when someone went to investigate, there were a lot of bad smells, but no weasels."

"That sounds bad," said Wilbur.

"No one could figure it out. So they sent word for me. I'm . . . uh . . . well, the other weasel-wolves know me." He ducked his head, looking faintly embarrassed. "A bit like you, Princess Harriet. I solve problems."

BY HITTING THEM WITH SWORDS?

"I do try to ask questions first," said Grey. "I mean, you'd hate to bite the wrong people."

"Naturally," said Harriet. Wilbur rolled his eyes.

"Anyway," said Grey, "I went to investigate.

There were some very weird smells, but no solid clues." He rubbed his nose again, as if it hurt. "Then the next pack began to report seeing someone in the woods."

"What sort of someone?" asked Harriet, by now quite interested.

Grey ran a hand through his fur. "A little girl," he said. "Dressed all in red. A hamster, like you—and me, during the full moon."

"Red!" said Harriet.

"Red?" said Wilbur doubtfully. "But she's a little girl. How dangerous can she be?"

DON'T BE FOOLED, WILBUR. LITTLE GIRLS ARE EXTREMELY DANGEROUS. I WAS ONE MYSELF ONCE.

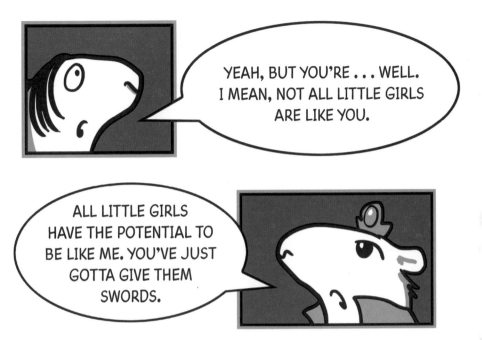

"She would just appear and stare at them," Grey continued. "And keep staring. They'd turn around, thinking they were completely alone, and there she'd be."

Harriet thought about being alone somewhere and then discovering a small girl in red was staring at you. That *did* seem pretty creepy. Harmless people didn't just show up and stare at you.

And Red had certainly had a strangely penetrating stare, as if she was trying to hypnotize someone.

"Did they try talking to her?" asked Wilbur.

Grey gave him a look. "How exactly were they supposed to do that? We're weasel-wolves. We don't speak Rodent. I mean, I do, because I'm a were-hamster, but most of them don't."

"Oh. Yeah, okay, that would be a problem . . ."

"One or two of them tried to eat her," said Grey, as if it were perfectly normal to try to eat people.

"That wasn't very nice," said Wilbur.

Grey looked blank. "Weasels gotta eat. And she was in their territory. What more did they want, a signed invitation?"

WE'VE REALLY GOT TO HAVE A TALK ABOUT ALL THIS EATING PEOPLE BUSINESS . . .

"Don't get hung up on irrelevant details, Wilbur," said Harriet. "What happened when they tried to eat her?"

Grey shook his head. "They said something happened. They didn't know what. Two of them attacked her. One says that the last thing he saw was her staring at him, and then he woke up an hour later. His packmate was gone. So was the little girl."

Wilbur rubbed the back of his neck and frowned.

IT'S NOT THAT I APPROVE OF EATING PEOPLE, BUT THAT *IS* PRETTY WEIRD . . .

"It gets worse," said Grey grimly. "The pack that

I talked to? A week later *all* of them disappeared."

"Whoa."

"My pack is the next one in line. And now she's shown up here," said Grey. "In that house on wheels."

"What about the grandmother?" asked Wilbur.

Grey shook his head. "No one's ever seen her. Just the strange little girl going in and out of the house."

"So you think she's responsible for the vanishings?" said Wilbur. "Red, I mean, not her grandmother. Well, maybe her grandmother too . . ."

IF SHE ISN'T, SHE'S CERTAINLY SHOWING UP UNDER SUSPICIOUS CIRCUMSTANCES.

Harriet gritted her teeth. She felt compelled to be fair. She hadn't liked Red very much, but Red was one of her subjects. And because she hadn't liked her, she knew that she had to try extra hard to be fair, because it would be so much easier for Harriet to believe something bad about her.

"I mean, it's very weird, but it doesn't prove anything."

"She's got a giant cage on wheels next to her house!"

Harriet had to admit that this was very suspicious indeed. "Do you think she's keeping were-weasels in it?"

Grey frowned. "There aren't any now," he admitted. "But why would you lug a giant cage around with you?"

That was an excellent question. Harriet put her head in her hands.

"Don't trust her," said Grey. "That's all."
"Red warned me not to trust you, either!"

BUT WHAT DOES *LYING* SMELL LIKE?

CAN'T HAMSTERS SMELL *ANYTHING?*

"I don't think we're going to sort this out with smells," said Wilbur gently.

Grey shook himself. "Look," he said. "I'm the toughest weasel-wolf in these woods."

He didn't say this as if he was bragging. He just said it as if it was true. It reminded Wilbur of the way that Harriet said she was the best warrior on the professional jousting circuit. The sky was blue, water was wet, Grey was the toughest weasel-wolf in the woods.

"But," Grey continued, "I don't want to risk my pack's lives on the chance that I'm not tough enough. That's why I sent you the note, Princess. That's why I'm talking to you now. I need your help figuring out who this little girl is and where my people are vanishing to."

Harriet clutched her head. "I don't know who to trust! I *don't* think you're lying. But if I'm wrong, it's a little girl and her grandmother that are in trouble, not just Wilbur and me!"

The fur on Grey's back stood up in spikes as if he were angry. But then it slowly smoothed back down again, and the were-hamster sighed.

"I understand," he said. "I have to be careful risking my pack too."

He stood up. "I'd decide who to trust soon,

Princess," he said. "Because more weasel-wolves may start vanishing, and if they do, I'm going to save them. Regardless of what—or who—stands in my way."

Harriet tried to think of something to say to that, but Grey melted away into the woods and one by one, the glowing eyes of the weasel-wolves vanished as they followed.

# CHAPTER 9

Harriet and Wilbur spent the hours until dawn arguing about what they should do next.

Harriet distrusted weasel-wolves in general, and were-weasel-wolves, presumably, were like weasel-wolves, only more so. But at the same time, she had liked Grey quite a lot, and she hadn't liked Red. So she found herself arguing both sides of the case, and as soon as Wilbur started to agree with her, she changed sides.

"Then we should trust Grey, because he said she kept showing up and staring at weasel-wolves."

"But Red told us not to trust anything he said!"

"Then don't trust her," said Wilbur.

"But she was acting really bizarre!"

"I thought she was nice. You're just suspicious of nice people."

"That's not true. I'm not suspicious of *you*."

Wilbur paused. This was almost a compliment. He savored it for a few seconds. "So don't trust Red, then."

"But Grey wants to eat her grandmother!"

Wilbur put his face in his hands. "I'm going to go to sleep," he said. "You're obviously capable of having this argument without my help."

"But—"

He curled up next to Hyacinth and pulled part of her wing over himself as a blanket.

Harriet attempted to argue with a tree for a while. It wasn't nearly as satisfying.

By morning, she was no closer to a decision. Obviously she should trust the little girl and her helpless grandmother over the were-hamster that ate people. *Obviously.*

And yet . . . and yet . . .

WERE-WEASELS ARE SUPPOSED TO BE DANGEROUS! TRICKY! NEARLY UNKILLABLE!

"Yeah, we don't know *anybody* like that . . ." muttered Wilbur.

"I heard that!" said Harriet. She couldn't really be offended, though—"dangerous," "tricky," and "nearly unkillable" were pretty nice things for someone to call you. "It's different. I mean, I don't *eat* people."

"Except the one time you almost—"

"We have been over that, Wilbur! If you sleep in a casserole dish, bad things are going to happen to you! No jury in the world would convict me!"

Mumfrey and Hyacinth exchanged meaningful looks.

"Are you afraid that you won't be able to fight off a were-weasel?" asked Wilbur.

I'LL FIGHT ANY WERE-WEASEL ON EARTH! I'LL FIGHT TEN OF THEM! WITH ONE HAND TIED BEHIND MY BACK! NO, BOTH HANDS!

"How are you going to hold your sword, then, if you've got your hands behind your back?"

"I will hold it in my teeth."

"Well," said Wilbur, after a few alarming minutes picturing Harriet holding a sword in her teeth. "I guess all we can do is go talk to Red's grandmother."

# CHAPTER 10

It was a short, uneventful trip to the clearing. No one was in evidence.

Harriet and Wilbur stood outside the wagon. The door was painted a cheerful blue.

"This is all so *normal*," whispered Wilbur.

"I know. Creepy, isn't it?" Harriet raised her fist and banged on the door.

"Who's there?" asked an old woman's voice.

"Princess Harriet! Open in the name of—well, me!"

"They don't usually ask 'who's there?' you know? They say 'Go away!' or 'We didn't do it!' or 'There are no monsters in here!'"

"People actually say *there are no monsters in here?*"

"Yeah. Especially the monsters. And they never open the door."

The door opened.

WELL, THERE'S A FIRST TIME FOR EVERYTHING . . .

The little girl in red looked at them. "Did you deal with the big weasel-wolf?"

"You mean Grey?"

"I mean the stinky awful weasel-wolf who eats people!" She stamped her foot again.

"Uh . . . I . . . talked to him . . ." said Harriet. "Why didn't you tell me he was a were-hamster? And we really need to have a word about this foot-stamping thing."

"You can't believe him!" said Red, going for

another foot stamp. "He wants to eat my grand-mother! And then I won't have anybody!"

"See, when you do that with the foot, people just stop taking you seriously. It's hard enough to get people to listen when you're under the age of—"

WHY DIDN'T YOU SLAY HIM!?

"Grey? It didn't seem like I needed to. He's just worried about . . ."

"Then go away!" shouted Red, and slammed the door.

". . . his pack," finished Harriet, looking at the door.

She could hear voices inside the wagon, too low to make out the words. The quail shifted restlessly, qwerking to themselves.

"Well, now what?" she said.

"Maybe we could get them together with a mediator?" said Wilbur.

"Maybe I could bash everyone over the head and throw them in a room and they can't leave until they've sorted this out."

Wilbur rubbed his forehead. Harriet had some very straightforward ideas about conflict resolution.

The wagon door opened.

Harriet looked at Wilbur. Wilbur looked at Harriet.

"This bit might be a trap," whispered Wilbur behind his hand.

"Gee, ya think?"

Nevertheless, Harriet stepped into the house.

The wagon was a single room, dominated by a large bed. It was dark and stiflingly hot inside. The only light came from the fireplace. Harriet felt her fur grow damp with sweat.

The little girl stepped aside. Harriet could see a lump in the blankets in the bed, where someone was lying.

"Come a little closer, my dear," said the person in the bed. She wore a white lace cap tied up under her chin and spoke with an old woman's voice, but Harriet didn't need Grey's sense of smell to know something strange was going on.

"You must be Grandmother," said Harriet.

"Oh yes. Please, come closer. I don't hear so well at my age . . ."

"How odd," said Harriet, taking a single step forward. "When you have such big ears." They were large and triangular and stuck up from either side of her cap.

"And what large hairy paws you have," said Wilbur worriedly. Grandmother's paws were enormous and knobbly and covered in gray fur.

"It's a skin condition," said Grandmother. "And it's a bit rude of you to comment. I'm very sensitive about it." She put her paws under the blanket.

"Sorry," said Wilbur. "I just . . . uh . . . sorry."

"It's all right, my dear," said Grandmother, smiling.

"My, what big teeth you have . . ." muttered Harriet.

"Oh come on!" shouted Harriet. "I don't mind having monsters lie to me, but anybody could tell you're a weasel-wolf!"

She grabbed the blanket on the bed and yanked it off. "Hey!" yelled Grandmother.

Underneath the blanket, Grandmother had a shaggy pelt. A long gray tail came out from under her nightgown.

"I'm not a weasel-wolf!" shouted the nightgown-clad weasel. "I'm a hamster! Weasel-wolves are horrible, nasty, awful monsters!"

Harriet scratched the back of her neck. "Ah . . . hmm. Okay, I can see there's some kind of really awkward psychology at work here, and normally I'd let Wilbur get to the bottom of it—tactfully—"

"It's what I do."

"—but weasel-wolves are vanishing and your granddaughter is wandering around in the woods staring at them—"

"Am not!" said Red.

"Don't tell fibs, dear," said Grandmother, yanking the blanket back over herself.

Red scuffed her toe on the floor. "Fine," she mumbled. "I might stare a little."

"And you have a very special stare, don't you, dear? I'm very proud of you."

Red beamed.

"But why are you staring at weasel-wolves?" said Harriet, baffled.

"It's the only way to catch them," said Red, as if Harriet were being rather slow.

"But why do you want to catch them?" asked Wilbur. "You said they were horrible and stinky!"

WE HAVE TO CATCH THEM, OF COURSE. AND THEN RED HYPNOTIZES THEM SO THEY THINK THEY'RE PETS. PEOPLE WON'T BUY THEM OTHERWISE.

# CHAPTER 11

*B*uy them?" said Harriet.

"They're great pets," said the little girl. "They're really sweet and loyal once they're hypnotized!"

"That's right," said Grandmother. "And my little Red is the best at catching them!"

She put her arm around Red. Red snuggled up against her grandmother, not seeming to notice the teeth and claws and fur.

"You can't sell the weasel-wolves as pets!" said Harriet, aghast.

"Why not? I've been doing it for months," said Grandmother. "It's worked fine so far."

"What's the problem?" said Grandmother. "Wild weasel-wolves are bad. The woods will be much safer once they're gone."

"But they live in the woods," said Wilbur, trying to sound calm and reasonable. "It's their home!"

"I don't care! It's my home too! I moved here a year ago, fair and square!"

Wilbur frowned. "But there have been weasel-wolves in the woods for as long as I've been alive . . ."

Grandmother yanked her blanket tighter around herself. "I'll fix that soon enough," she said.

"They're really nice pets!" said Red. "They're sweet and they don't scare anyone and once you give them a couple of baths, they don't stink at all."

"And they don't bite anyone," added Grandmother. "Everybody's happier. Happy weasels, happy customers, happy . . . err . . . people not getting eaten in the woods . . ."

BUT . . .

"After we're all done, Grandmother says I get to keep one!" said Red happily. "There's a little tiny one in the woods who is so cute!"

"And if you decide you don't want him, we'll sell him as a teacup weasel for twice the price!" said Grandmother.

It was impossible for Harriet to put her thoughts into words—fighting a hungry weasel-wolf that came after you in the woods was one thing, but hypnotizing them to be pets was entirely different.

She suspected that Grey would not be happy at all to hear about what was happening to his pack.

"The big weasel-wolf—" she began.

The little girl folded her arms. "That's why we need your help! He's been sniffing around and he's actually scary!"

"You're kidnapping his friends!" said Wilbur.

"I'm running a small independent business!" said Grandmother.

"You're running a small independent business

that specializes in kidnapping his friends and selling them as pets!" shouted Harriet. "Of course he's trying to stop you!"

Grandmother scowled with all her sharp weasel-wolf teeth. "You know, I had hoped that a princess would be more concerned about her subjects!"

"I'm very concerned!" shouted Harriet.

I'M CONCERNED THAT YOU'RE KIDNAPPING THEM AND SELLING THEM!

Even Wilbur gave her a surprised look. "Does

this mean the weasel-wolves are your subjects?" he whispered.

Harriet gritted her teeth. She'd fought weasel-wolves on multiple occasions and they were scary and they did eat people and . . .

And . . .

And it just wasn't okay that they were being sold as pets, and that was all there was to it.

"I can see you're going to be unreasonable about this," said Grandmother. She sighed. "I *did* hope we'd be able to come to an understanding. I suppose we'll have to move, and just after I got settled. Little Red, my dear, you know what to do."

Red threw her hood back and stared Harriet in the face.

"What?" said Harriet.

Harriet tried to look away, but there was something strange going on. Something very strange. Red's hypnotic eyes seemed to fill the entire world. Harriet tried to grab her sword, but it felt as if she were moving through molasses.

Her last thought was that now she understood why the wolves had gotten out of Red's way, and that she had to find some way to tell Grey what he was up against.

# CHAPTER 12

Harriet yawned and woke up. There was a weasel-wolf standing over her, jaws on the collar of her jacket, dragging her somewhere.

Her first instinct was to swing her fist at it, since it was probably trying to eat her, but then she remembered what was happening.

"Easy," said a familiar voice.

"Grey?" said Harriet. "Is that you?" Her head was splitting. She sat up and rubbed the base of her ears. "Where's Wilbur?"

"I've got him."

"Is he all right?" said Harriet.

"He's pretty groggy . . ."

"'M fine," mumbled Wilbur as Grey set him down. "Just . . . ow. My brain feels scrambled. I think I fainted."

"What happened to you two?"

"It was Red," said Harriet. "She stared at us. No, not like you're staring at me. Like . . . her eyes did a thing. A whirly swirly thing. And then I fell over."

FAINTED.

Harriet abandoned this line of conversation for a more important one. "How did you get us out of Grandmother's wagon?"

"I didn't," said Grey. "You were both lying on the ground. Your quail were very upset and qwerking like anything."

"Qwerk!" cried Mumfrey, who had been pacing back and forth in the background. "Qwerk qwerk!" This was Quail for "I didn't know how to wake you up, so I went and got the big weasel-wolf. He's a weasel, but at least he has thumbs."

"Qwerk," added Hyacinth, which was Quail for "I still don't trust him, but thumbs are really useful."

"Where's the wagon?" asked Harriet, jumping to her feet. "Red's the one who's been stealing your people! You were right, Grey!"

He looked like he wanted to say more, but the tiny weasel-wolf they had seen earlier dashed up and began to woof frantically at Grey.

"Uh-oh," said Grey.

"Uh-oh-what?" said Wilbur. He didn't like "uh-oh." When Harriet said "uh-oh" it usually meant that everything was on fire, the floor was about to collapse, and her mother was getting home early and about to see the mess she'd made.

"This is Snuffle. He was hiding, and the little girl went by him. And then one of his packmates chased after her. And didn't come back."

Harriet thought quickly. If Grandmother was selling the weasel-wolves as pets, Snuffle's packmate might be in grave danger indeed.

"We've got to get back to those wagons!"

Snuffle gulped and tried to hide behind Grey. Grey sighed. "Yes, but . . . uh . . ."

"He's scared of Harriet, isn't he?" said Wilbur.

WHAT? ME? WHY? I'M NOT EVEN POINTING MY SWORD AT HIM!

She waved her sword around for emphasis. Snuffle let out a yelp and dove behind Wilbur.

". . . I'll walk in back," said Harriet, sighing.

"That's not the only thing," said Grey. "It's . . . well, look for yourself." He pointed through the woods.

Harriet followed in the direction he'd pointed and saw the clearing.

There were huge ruts in the grass where the wheels had passed. Other than that, the clearing was empty.

The wagons were gone.

# CHAPTER 13

This is a problem," said Harriet.

"If they've left my territory, I'd normally be glad to just let them go," said Grey. "But they've taken Shaggy Paw."

"Shaggy Paw?"

"Snuffle's friend."

Harriet sighed. "Yeah, and they're gonna sell him as a pet."

THEY WHAT.

Wilbur and Snuffle hid behind Harriet. Harriet tilted her head to one side and waited while Grey howled in rage.

The were-hamster's chest was heaving with outrage. "A pet? She's selling my people as *pets?*"

"And we're going to stop them!" snapped Harriet. "Focus, Grey!"

Grey blinked at her. Then he turned his back and took several deep breaths.

"You're right," he said, after a minute. "I'll get mad later." He took a deep breath. "But I'm going to get *really* mad."

"Totally fair." Harriet was rather interested to see what that would look like. For a minute there, Grey had looked exactly as savage and dangerous as the legends of were-weasels said they were.

Snuffle whimpered. Wilbur petted him behind the ears. The tiny weasel-wolf looked sad and frightened.

"We'll get your friend back," promised Wilbur.

"Wrrflle . . ."

"Okay," said Harriet. "First things first. Let's find those wagons!"

"The woods are lovely, dark, and deep . . ." said Wilbur. They were walking single file through the woods in question. Shafts of early morning light cut through the trees around them. The weasel-wolves were all hanging back, but Wilbur no longer found their glowing eyes particularly alarming.

It was probably because of Snuffle. Snuffle was the opposite of alarming. Wilbur, never the most physically imposing of hamsters, had a strong urge to hug Snuffle and tell him that everything was going to be okay.

"This is no time for poetry, Wilbur," said Harriet. "We gotta find Snuffle's friend before they sell him."

"I'm still wondering how they're moving the wagons," said Wilbur. "No quail. No draft chickens. They'd have to be enormously strong. Or use magic, I guess."

"Unless they're fairies," mused Harriet. "Sometimes fairies do that thing where they go 'poof!' and there's sparkly bits and then they're somewhere else. It's really annoying."

"Wrrf?" said Snuffle.

"Makes your nose itch."

"Wrrf!"

PROBABLY NOT, THOUGH. SHE DIDN'T HAVE THAT FAIRY LOOK. MORE OF A GIANT DROOL-Y WEASEL-HAMSTER HYBRID LOOK.

"Wrrfffl!?"

"Yeah, it was pretty weird.

"I wonder . . ." she said.

"What?"

"What if the grandmother's pulling the wagon? Aren't were-weasels supposed to be much stronger than usual?"

IF SHE'S THAT STRONG, HOW ARE YOU GOING TO FIGHT HER?

PFF, I'VE FOUGHT GIANTS. I FOUGHT A GIANT LAST *MONTH.*

"Although . . ." said Harriet thoughtfully, "you know, if Grey would turn me into a were-weasel, I'd be just as strong as she is . . ."

Wilbur hastily changed the subject. "I don't know why she's so mad at weasels if she's one herself. And then she's turning around and selling them!"

"Maybe she was selling them before and then one bit her," said Harriet. "During the—what was it? The Changes?"

Grey nodded. "That might do it. Although I don't know why she hates us so much. She said we smelled bad!"

"Hey, your drawing of *me* had stink-lines," said Harriet, who had been meaning to bring that up for a while.

"Of course it did," said Grey. "You smell strong. Like a warrior!"

Wilbur put his hand over his mouth and made a strangled noise.

"I do?" said Harriet.

"Definitely. You smell like defeated enemies. Well, and quail."

The noises coming from behind Wilbur's hand were getting louder as he tried not to laugh in Harriet's face.

"Qwerk," said Mumfrey, which was Quail for "I've never noticed it."

"Yes, but you're a quail," said Harriet. "Quail don't have a very good sense of smell." Mumfrey looked vaguely offended.

"It's a good thing," Grey tried to assure her. "The lines were complimentary. Only a powerful warrior would have such stink-lines!"

Wilbur lost it.

Harriet leaned against a tree and waited for her friend to recover. It took a few minutes.

"Are you quite done?" she asked finally.

"Ah . . . ha . . . hee . . . heh-heh . . . I think so." Wilbur wiped his eyes. "Sorry, Harriet . . ."

"It's fine," said Harriet, who was feeling intensely torn between a desire to go shower and pride at her powerful warrior stink-lines.

Meanwhile, Snuffle had been sniffing through the undergrowth. He came back to tug at Grey's hand.

"Snuffle says the trail keeps going," said Grey. "And they're moving slower now."

"Does he smell Shaggy Paw?"

Snuffle screwed up his face. "Faintly, he thinks," translated Grey. "He's not sure."

"We might be able to catch up to them," said Harriet, "if *some* people can stop giggling . . ."

"I can walk and laugh at the same time," said Wilbur.

They hurried through the undergrowth after Snuffle. Snuffle had his nose down and was trotting along rapidly, making little "wrrf-wrrf-wrrf" noises to himself.

He began to pick up speed. Harriet broke into a jog. If Snuffle went much faster, they'd have to stop and get on the quail in order to keep up with the little weasel-wolf.

And then . . .

"Wrrf . . . wrrf . . . *GAAAAH!*"

# CHAPTER 14

Snuffle threw himself backward so violently that he did a full somersault and lay flat on the ground, sneezing thunderously. Grey stopped just as short. Harriet ran into his back. Wilbur ran into Harriet. Mumfrey threw out his wings to either side and managed to brake before he fell over the hamsters completely.

"Aaahhhchooo!"

"What happened?" asked Harriet.

Harriet sniffed the air. Now that she was pay-
ing attention, she *could* smell something. It was a

faint but unpleasant powdery perfume, the sort that her great-aunt Snizzy would wear. (Snizzy was extremely uptight and concerned with lady-like behavior, and Harriet would have disliked her anyway, but the fact that she always smelled like a hothouse full of dying flowers didn't help.)

"Why is there *perfume* in the *woods?*" asked Harriet.

"They must have known we were following them," said Grey grimly. "So they dumped out a bottle of perfume." He held his paws over his nose. "Gnnnrggh. Oh, that's nasty!"

"You don't like perfume, but you like warrior stink?" said Wilbur.

"Don't start," warned Harriet. "And can you smell it?"

Wilbur went over to where poor Snuffle had been and inhaled. "Okay, yeah . . . this is kind of nasty. But why dump out perfume? Wouldn't that just make them easier to follow by smell?"

"Snuffle won't be following anybody for a bit," said Grey glumly. "Poor guy got a full nose of it. It's like . . . oh, like throwing sand in somebody's eyes so they can't see you."

AH-CHOO!

Neither Snuffle nor Grey could get past the perfume bomb. Harriet tried to track by scent, but she couldn't even smell the perfume after going about ten feet. Grey tried to help, got a whiff, and started sneezing violently.

"Qwerk," said Mumfrey, which was Quail for "Like you said about the sense of smell . . ."

"I think we've been defeated for the moment," said Wilbur.

Harriet scowled, but she had to admit that he was right. Grey's eyes and nose were streaming and they had to put poor Snuffle on Mumfrey's back, since he could barely walk.

When they were out of range of the scent, Wilbur pulled a box of tissues out of Hyacinth's pack. Grey and Snuffle sat next to each other, wiping their noses and sneezing.

AH...
AHH...
AHHH...

"So what's our next move?" asked Wilbur.

Grey shook his head. "I don't—achoo!—know. If I can't track them, I can't fight them."

"We'll have to catch the little girl in the act," said Harriet. "Even if she throws perfume, Mumfrey and I will still be able to follow her."

"How are we going to do that?" asked Wilbur. "She obviously knows we're trying to catch her. Won't she be more careful this time?"

Harriet tapped her nail against her teeth. "Probably. So we're going to have to set a trap."

"A—achoo!—ahhhh-CHOO!—trap?"

Harriet nodded. "But we're going to need bait. She takes lone weasel-wolves, right? She didn't try to go for the whole pack when we were together. So what we need is a weasel-wolf so helpless, so harmless, that this junior mastermind has to pounce."

She turned and looked and began to smile.

"And she said that there was one weasel in the forest that her grandmother would let her keep as a pet . . ."

"Wrrff?" said Snuffle.

# CHAPTER 15

They had to wait until both the weasel-wolves had stopped sneezing, which took some doing. But finally their noses seemed to settle down. Harriet rolled to her feet. "All right. Let's set the trap!"

"Snuffle's a little worried," admitted Grey.

"I won't let that weird kid harm a hair on Snuffle's head," said Harriet. "My word as a warrior."

Grey woofed to Snuffle, who *wrrgll*'d back. "He says that if it'll help get Shaggy Paw back, he'll try to be brave."

"For this to work, Snuffle needs to be the only target," said Harriet. "The rest of the pack needs to hide."

Grey frowned. "If I knew a place where they'd be safe, I wouldn't have to worry about this kid weasel-napping them!"

"No problem," said Harriet. "They can go to my castle. Let me write a note to my mom . . ."

"Dear Mom & Dad," Harriet wrote. "I am sending you these weasel-wolves. They are a pack. The pack leader is a friend of mine. They need a place to stay where they will not be captured. Please take care of them."

She chewed on the end of her pencil for a moment. Should she add anything else? What did weasel-wolves eat?

"Grasshoppers," said Grey, when she asked. "About the size of your thumb. And lizards—not like people's pet lizards, the little snappy ones— and things like that, mostly."

I THOUGHT YOU MOSTLY ATE PEOPLE . . .

IF WE HAD TO WAIT FOR SOMEBODY TO WANDER INTO THE WOODS IN ORDER TO EAT, WE'D ALL BE A LOT THINNER.

"You eat *grasshoppers?*" said Harriet.
"Sure. Don't you?"
". . . not usually, no."

"Oh. You should try it. There's good eating on a grasshopper."

"Qwerk!" said Mumfrey, which was Quail for "He's right, you know."

Harriet shrugged and added a P.S. to the letter that said, "They eat grasshoppers and lizards and sometimes people."

"Are you sure it's safe?" said Wilbur doubtfully. "They won't just see weasel-wolves and attack first?"

"I'm not sure what else to do," admitted Harriet.

"We could send Hyacinth. Then they'd know they were friendly."

"Qwerrkk . . ." said Hyacinth. She looked from Grey to the weasel-wolves, then to Wilbur. "Qwerk!" she said, which was Quail for "I'm a little scared, but I could be brave if the weasels promise not to eat me."

"If you do this for us," said Grey, "I promise that no weasel-wolf of my pack will ever hunt you again, from now to the end of the world."

Hyacinth pulled herself up until she looked every bit as proud as a peacock. "Qwerk," she said.

The pack crept toward her, bowing very low. "Wrrf," said Snuffle.

Her head held high, topknot bouncing, Hyacinth led the way back toward the castle, with an honor guard of weasel-wolves on either side.

# CHAPTER 16

This is the place where Shaggy Paw disappeared yesterday," said Grey, stopping. Harriet didn't know how he could tell one chunk of dark woods from another, but she took his word for it.

"All right," she said. "Snuffle, can you . . . um . . . frolic in the woods or something?"

. . . WRRF?

"Frolic!" said Harriet. "You know! Like—um— bounce around and attract attention. Sniff butter- flies. Pretend you don't have a care in the world."

Snuffle looked at her as if she'd lost her mind. Fortunately, people were always giving Harriet this look, so it didn't bother her.

"We're going to be in this tree," said Harriet. "You sit here where she can see you. And if Red comes back, we'll be right above you."

They all piled up onto Mumfrey, hanging on opposite sides of the saddle. It was very uncomfortable, but Mumfrey was a strong quail. He took a deep breath, then leaped upward, flapping wildly.

He caught the lowest branch of the tree, scrambled upright, and locked his talons into the bark.

"That was great, Mumfrey!" said Harriet.

"Qwerk."

"You can open your eyes now, Wilbur."

"I'd rather not."

"Now what happens?" asked Grey.

Harriet cracked her knuckles. "Now we wait."

To give Snuffle the credit he deserved, he tried to frolic. He really tried.

He rolled around on the ground, chased his own tail, gathered flowers—there weren't really any flowers deep in the woods, so he gathered pine needles and made a rather pointy bouquet out of them. Then he chased his tail some more.

"And this is supposed to convince the creepy little girl in red to kidnap him?" asked Grey dubiously.

"You don't think she'll fall for it?"

"I think she'll be afraid he's got *rabies*."

"Nah, he'd be foaming at the mouth."

"If he keeps trying to put pine needles up his nose, it may happen."

"I'm sure it'll be—*aha!*"

From their perch in the tree, Harriet could see Red approaching through the woods. She slapped her hand over Grey's mouth and pointed.

Snuffle continued attempting to frolic.

Red came up to the bushes on the edge of the clearing where Snuffle was chasing his tail. She watched him with a doubtful expression on her face.

Snuffle managed to catch his tail in his mouth and then seemed baffled as to what to do with it.

The hamster girl fought back a smile.

Then her smile faded. She sighed and shook her head and stepped into the clearing.

"Hi," said the little girl. "You're kind of cute, aren't you? You're the cute little one I keep seeing."

"Blrrfle?"

"I guess I have to do this," she said. She pushed her hood back and narrowed her eyes. Snuffle started backing away, but he still had his tail in his mouth, so he went sideways and nearly fell over.

"Aww, you're so cute," said the little girl. "You're not big and scary like the others. But Grandmother says we can't leave any of you wandering around. And she did say that I could keep one as a pet."

The little weasel-wolf's eyes went wide. Then Red crouched down and began to stare.

Snuffle panicked. But instead of running away or attacking, he threw his fluffy tail over his eyes and cowered.

"Don't be scared," said the little girl, reaching out and petting Snuffle behind the ears. "It won't hurt at all! But how am I supposed to do this if you've got your tail over your face?"

"Wrrfl!"

Red sat down. "It's okay! You'll like being a pet weasel, I promise! All the weasel-wolves are much happier after I hypnotize them. And I'll take good care of you and we'll be friends forever."

"Wrrfllll . . ."

She heaved an enormous sigh. "Moving around all the time isn't fun. I don't have any friends, just Grandmother. She said I could finally keep one of the weasel-wolves, though, and I thought maybe you'd like to be my friend?"

Red sniffled, sounding like she might cry.
"Awww . . ." whispered Wilbur.

The other two looked at him. Grey said, "What? It's sad that she's sad, but she's selling my people as pets!"

"You can't just eat people!" hissed Wilbur. "Particularly not if they're sad!"

"Yes, but if I eat her, then no one will be sad. It's win-win!"

*"Nobody gets eaten."*

"Is he always like this?" whispered Grey to Harriet.

"Frequently."

Down on the ground, Snuffle had slowly moved his tail in response to Red's tears. He was a very compassionate little weasel-wolf. He leaned over and licked Red's face.

She jumped, startled. "Eep!"

"Eep!" said Snuffle, and threw his tail back over his eyes.

"You startled me!"

"Wrrfl?"

"I still think we should eat her," muttered Grey.

"I don't want to scare you," said Red. "Grandmother says weasel-wolves are dumb, so it doesn't matter what we do to them, but—"

This was too much for Harriet's sense of fairness.

YOU CAN'T TREAT PEOPLE LIKE THAT JUST BECAUSE YOU THINK THEY'RE DUMB!

Red looked up and gasped.

"Wrrr!" cried Snuffle, reaching for her, but the little girl took off at a run.

"After her!" shouted Harriet. "Mumfrey, get us down!"

Grey didn't even bother trying to ride the quail down. He just jumped.

Mumfrey leaped out of the tree with Harriet and Wilbur clinging to him. Harriet flung herself out of the saddle and after Grey. "Wilbur, get Snuffle!" she yelled over her shoulder, and took off at a run after Grey.

Branches whipped at her and leaves slapped her in the face, but Harriet didn't care. She was a hamster, which isn't a species built for speed, but so was the little girl, so presumably it evened out. She had to catch up!

She made it about ten yards into the woods and then heard an explosive sneeze.

"Gaaagghhhchooo!" Grey fell down practically at her feet. He seemed to be experiencing a full-body sneeze.

"Grey? Grey, are you okay?"

"Per—per—AACCHOOO!"

Harriet didn't need to ask for details. The heavy, cloying smell of perfume was so thick that she could smell it too.

Still, it was just sneezing and Grey would be fine. The important thing was not to lose the trail. Harriet vaulted over the sneezing were-hamster and charged onward.

Her legs were longer than the little girl's, if not by much. (No hamster is ever particularly long-legged.) If it hadn't been so dark, she could have caught her. As it was, she would lose track for an instant, then see the red cloak through the trees, lit by occasional patches of moonlight.

She plunged into a thicket of ferns and lost Red completely for a minute. As she floundered, she heard the sound of running feet.

Mumfrey slid up beside her. Grey was draped across the quail's back, still sneezing weakly. Wilbur was holding Snuffle in his lap and trying to hold on to Mumfrey. "That way!" he yelled, pointing.

Harriet charged in that direction and caught another glimpse of red.

The trees seemed to open up in front of them. Quail and hamsters burst into the clearing.

# CHAPTER 17

Grandmother had clearly relocated her wheeled wagon to this clearing. It looked exactly as it had the last time Harriet had seen it, with one major exception.

Inside the wheeled cage was a sleeping weasel-wolf. His paws were crossed and his head was down. Harriet could hear faint snoring sounds coming from his direction.

"Shaggy Paw!" said Grey.

"Wrrfl!" said Snuffle.

"Gah!" Red stamped her foot.

"What did I say about that?" said Harriet, advancing toward the little girl. "You've got to lay off the foot-stamping. Nobody takes you seriously!"

"I am taking her seriously," said Wilbur.

"Yes, but—"

Red pushed her hood back and stared at Harriet.

Harriet had her hand over her eyes and was feeling her way forward blindly when she heard a loud *slam.*

"You can probably look now," said Wilbur. "She ran inside the wagon."

Harriet lowered her hand, feeling a bit silly. "Fighting people who can hypnotize you is always hard. If I'd known she could do that, I'd have brought a mirror or something."

"A mirror?"

"Yeah, that's how you fight basilisks and gorgons and things that turn you to stone by staring at you. It's just hard because you have to swing your sword in reverse and it's easy to get mixed up."

"She didn't seem much like a gorgon," said Wilbur doubtfully. "Don't those usually have snakes for fur?"

"Oh, you know how it is, Wilbur. Somebody's great-aunt's a gorgon and they seem totally normal except that if they get into a bad mood, they accidentally petrify people. Sometimes this stuff skips generations."

"Like how *your* parents are completely normal," agreed Wilbur.

"Yes, exactly like—hey!"

"Wrrfl!" On the far side of the clearing, Snuffle was dancing around the cage, making worried noises. "Wrll??"

"He won't wake up," translated Grey. "There's something wrong—and what's he wearing?"

"Wearing?"

Harriet stepped in closer and lifted Shaggy Paw's head. Under his thick fur, she could see the outline of a collar.

"You don't put collars on us!" said Grey, sounding really angry. "We aren't pets!"

*"Wrrrll!"* Snuffle let out a noise of distress.

166

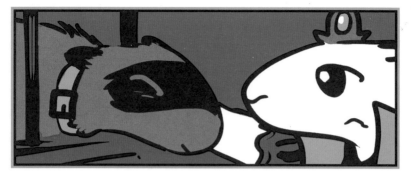

"Even if he does wake up," said Wilbur, "how are we going to get him out of this cage?"

They looked dubiously at the cage. There were chains wrapped around the door and a padlock as thick around as Wilbur's thumb.

"I can't chew through chains," said Harriet.

Grey grabbed the bars and pulled. Muscles strained under his fur.

The bars remained unbent. Even when Harriet tried to help, the cage was too strong.

"Or we could just find the key, maybe?" said Wilbur as the two hamsters collapsed, gasping.

"It would have been much cooler if we could bend the bars," muttered Harriet.

"That would have been awesome," muttered Grey.

Wilbur put his head in his hands. Being Harriet's sidekick was hard enough. If he had known that he'd have to wrangle *two* warrior hamsters, both determined to find the most aggressive route through the world, he'd have eaten a much bigger breakfast.

"While I'm as worried about Shaggy Paw as anyone," said Wilbur, "can I point out that he's not going anywhere, and there's a hypnotist little girl and her were-weasel grandmother in that wagon *right this minute?*"

"Wrrfl," grumbled Snuffle.

"You're right," said Grey. "But how are we going to get into the wagon?"

"Somehow I don't think they'll respond to a polite knock this time," said Harriet.

NOW, IF I HAD MY AX, WE WOULDN'T *NEED* A DOOR.

IT ALWAYS COMES BACK TO AXES WITH YOU.

"Hey, I took a safety class!"

While Snuffle stayed with Shaggy Paw, the hamsters approached the wagon cautiously. It was such a normal-looking house, except for the wheels. You expected the inhabitants to be baking cookies, not masterminding a weasel-wolf smuggling ring.

"I smell something weird," said Grey. "It smells almost like *me*."

"What?"

"Not like me, *personally*, but like a were-hamster. Except it isn't right for a were-hamster either."

"Oh," said Harriet. "That's the grandmother, I bet. You know how you look like a hamster that's sort of weasely?"

"Yes . . . ?"

"She looked like a weasel that was sort of hamstery. So I figure she must be like you, only from the opposite direction. Like I'll be if you bite me."

"Are you sure you want that?"

"Uh, *yeah!*" Harriet wrinkled her nose. "I'll be way better at it! I won't do anything silly like wandering around in a stupid nightgown trying to pretend I'm not a weasel-wolf."

"I can hear you, you know!" shouted Grandmother from inside the wagon. "And my nightgown is not stupid!"

Harriet made a fist and knocked on the door.

"Go away!" shouted Red.

"Let me in!" said Harriet.

"I won't!" shouted Red.

"She won't!" shouted Red's grandmother.

"Let me in! Or I'll . . . err . . . I'll huff and I'll puff and I'll—"

"I think that's supposed to be my line," said Grey.

"Have you ever blown a house down?"

"Honestly, it's never come up."

Harriet pounded on the door again.

"I'm not letting you in!" shouted Red.

"Well, I'm not going away!"

"Then we're at an impasse!" shouted Grandmother.

GAH! JUST ONCE, I WANT TO BE THE ONE WHO GETS TO SAY "WE'RE AT AN IMPASSE." JUST ONCE. BUT THE MONSTERS ALWAYS GET THERE FIRST.

"Can you hack through the door with your sword?" asked Grey.

"Why would I break a perfectly good sword doing that?"

They took a step back from the wagon and glared at it.

And then, quite suddenly, Harriet had an idea.

# CHAPTER 18

Maybe we can blow her house down! You guys know how a swing set works?" said Harriet.

"Yes," said Wilbur.

"No," said Grey.

"Qwerk," said Mumfrey, which was Quail for "Nobody makes swing sets for quail, and that makes me sad."

"Okay. You push in one direction, right? And then you pump your legs in the other direction. And the swing goes further each time."

"Wagons aren't swings," said Wilbur doubtfully.

"No, but the laws of physics still apply!" said Harriet, and putting her back against the side of the wagon, she began to push.

The wagon rocked to one side. As soon as it began to rock back, Harriet stopped pushing, then threw her weight against it as it went in the original direction.

Grey and Wilbur looked at each other doubtfully, shrugged, and put their backs against the wagon.

"Hey!" shouted Grandmother from inside. "What are you doing?!"

COME OUT OR WE'LL KNOCK YOUR HOUSE OVER!

The three hamsters kept rocking the cage back and forth between them. Mumfrey bounced on his claws, trying to use his strong wings to help.

The wagon wheels began to creak violently.

"There we go!" said Harriet. "It's almost one-fourth of the way over!"

"Oh, here we go with the fractions . . ." muttered Wilbur.

"Stop!" yelled Grandmother. "Stop it!"

"Come out!" shouted Harriet.

"You're a terrible person!" screamed Grandmother.

"But—an—excellent—princess—!" panted Harriet, flinging herself against the wagon. She could hear things sliding around inside the wagon and the crash of breaking crockery.

Snuffle abandoned the cage and came to help as best he could, although he kept trying to bite the wagon.

"One-third!" gasped Harriet. "Maybe two-fifths!"

The door flew open. Red flung herself out, followed by the hairy figure of Grandmother.

"Hraaaawwrrrroooof!" snarled Grey, abandoning the wagon. "You! You're the monster who's been selling my packmates!"

"I'm not a monster!" screamed Grandmother. *"You're* the monster!"

"But weasel-wolves aren't mon—" began Wilbur.

"Yes they are!" screamed Grandmother. Little flecks of spit rained down as she yelled.

I WASN'T ALWAYS A WERE-WEASEL! THIS MAY COME AS A SHOCK, BUT IT WAS ONE OF THOSE MONSTERS THAT TURNED ME INTO *THIS!*

She posed dramatically, but this revelation fell rather flat.

"Well, yeah," said Harriet. "That's how it happens, isn't it? Is anybody surprised?"

"Nope," said Wilbur.

"Qwerk."

"Wrrfl."

"Well—well—now I'm stuck like this!" ranted the obviously-a-were-weasel. "Every full moon I turn into a monster!"

It was ironic, Wilbur thought, that Harriet would probably give her left arm for the chance to turn into a were-weasel, and here Grandmother seemed very upset about it. Possibly this said something about attitude.

"Look," said Harriet. "Give us the key to the cage and turn yourself in and we don't have to do this the hard way."

"Grrrwwwooofff," growled Grey, who clearly was hoping to do it the hard way.

"I worked too hard to build a successful small business to give up now!"

Harriet drew her sword.

Grey charged.

Most people would look frightened when a giant slavering were-hamster ran at them, teeth flashing. Grandmother just looked irritated.

"Red," she said.

The hamster girl stepped fearlessly between Grey and her grandmother. Harriet expected her to try to hypnotize the were-hamster, which seemed very risky, given the speed at which Grey was traveling.

But instead, Red reached into the basket slung over her arm and pulled out a handful of . . . something.

She flung the handful directly into Grey's face.

*Glitter?* thought Harriet. *Sure, boys often act like they're terrified of glitter, and it gets in* everything, *but it's harmless; surely that wouldn't stop a charging . . .*

Grey let out a high-pitched yelp and folded up as if he'd struck a wall.

Ah.

Not glitter after all.

*Silver.*

# CHAPTER 19

Y ou threw silver on him!?" cried Harriet.

"Powdered silver," said Grandmother. "And it costs a fortune too. This whole thing is really cutting into my bottom line." She glared at Harriet, then over at Snuffle. "We're going to have to sell that little one as a teacup weasel for ten times the price."

Red looked up, her eyebrows drawing together. "But I don't want you to sell him, Grandmother! He's sweet!"

"Sorry, dear, but business comes first."

"But—"

"Mumfrey!" shouted Harriet. "Protect Snuffle!"

"Qwerk!" cried Mumfrey, spreading his wings over the tiny weasel-wolf.

SOMEONE'S GOT TO STOP YOUR REIGN OF TERROR, GRANDMOTHER!

Red straightened from over the prone Grey and stared at Harriet.

"Gaaah!" Harriet squinted, trying to fight her way through the hypnotic stare.

"I don't want to do this!" said Red.

"I don't want you to do it, either!" said Harriet, staggering forward.

"I . . . I . . ."

"You know this isn't right!" said Harriet. "Selling the weasel-wolves as pets! They have families and friends! You don't put collars on people!"

Red buried her face in her hands, sniffling. Freed from the terrible hypnotic stare, Harriet nearly fell. She was seeing double, or maybe triple. There were at least three Reds, a couple of Mumfreys, and a whole bunch of Grandmothers holding Wilbur in the middle of the clearing.

*"Wilbur!"*

"No funny business, Princess!" snapped Grandmother. "Or I'm gonna bite your little friend here and turn him into a monster!"

"Aw, *maaaan. . . .*" said Harriet, stepping forward. "Wilbur! When you're a were-weasel, you have to promise to make me one too!"

Harriet took another step forward. "C'mon, Wilbur, it'll be great! We can spend the full moon being weasels!"

Grandmother's enormous hairy eyebrows drew down. "What kind of weird princess are you?!"

THE AWESOME KIND!

"You're nuts," said Grandmother. "Look at me! You *want* to be like this?" She flung her arms open. Long, wiry hair hung out of the wrists and neck of the nightgown, and her cap was askew on her head. Wilbur dangled at the end of her clawed hand.

Harriet took two more steps forward. "You don't look so bad," she said. "I mean, the nightgown really is stupid but—YAAAAAAH!"

She pounced.

Harriet slammed into Grandmother's shoulder first, knocking the old were-weasel to the floor. Wilbur yelped, but her grip had loosened. He tore himself free and scurried across the clearing.

Snuffle, clearly frightened by the commotion, dove behind him.

"Wrrf! Wrrf! Wrrrrffflle!"

"You said it. Probably," said Wilbur.

Red drew closer, clutching her hood. "She won't hurt Grandmother, will she?"

"Your grandmother's supposed to be immortal except for silver weapons," Wilbur pointed out.

"Yes, but she gets really cross when people try to fight her."

There was a scream of rage from the center of the clearing. Apparently Grandmother was feeling rather cross right now.

YOU—HORRIBLE—LITTLE—PRINCESS!

Harriet dealt Grandmother a fearsome blow with her sword that would have stopped any lesser monster. Grandmother rolled over twice and jumped to her feet, looking none the worse for wear.

Harriet remembered that weasel-wolves were extremely tough. This had seemed more positive when she'd wanted to be one herself.

"I'm scared!" said Red, grabbing Wilbur's hand.

"Wrrfl!" said Snuffle, grabbing Wilbur's other hand.

I...UH...

He didn't know whom to comfort first. "Do you think maybe you could hug each other?" he asked. "I feel like I should be helping Harriet."

Wilbur carefully disentangled himself and put Snuffle's paw in Red's hand. The two looked at each other with wide eyes.

"You were the cute little one," said Red. "I didn't mean to scare you."

"Rwwffll-wfff!"

Wilbur didn't speak Weasel, but he could venture a guess. "You kidnapped his packmates," he said. "He was trying to find them."

GRANDMOTHER TOLD ME I HAD TO . . . I DIDN'T KNOW THEY HAD FRIENDS. AND I TRIED TO HYPNOTIZE THEM SO THEY WOULDN'T MIND OR BE SCARED AT ALL . . .

Across the clearing, Grandmother was driving Harriet back, step by step. Fighting a more-or-less invincible were-weasel by yourself was unexpectedly difficult when you didn't have an also more-or-less invincible were-hamster helping you. Harriet blocked claws and teeth with her sword, but now it was Grandmother's turn to drive her backward, inch by inch.

Her back hit the bars of the cage with the sleeping Shaggy Paw.

"You have to stop doing this!" yelled Harriet. "You're kidnapping innocent weasel-wolves!"

"They aren't innocent!" shouted Grandmother. "They're monsters!"

NO, *YOU'RE* A MONSTER! AND NOT BECAUSE YOU'RE A WERE-WEASEL!

"Wilbur!" she yelled. "Get everybody out of here!"

Wilbur looked at Red and Snuffle, who were apparently having a very deep heart-to-heart conversation despite the lack of a common language. He looked at Grey, who was unconscious, with wisps of smoke curling from his fur.

". . . I won't do it . . ." whispered Red in a very small voice.

"I don't know how to get them out of here!" said Wilbur. "I can't carry everybody!"

"You leave them right where they are!" snapped Grandmother. "I'm going to put a spiked collar on the big one and make him my personal guard-weasel! So he can keep the next meddling princess out of my business!"

She slashed her claws at Harriet. Harriet blocked one, ducked under the other—and felt her sword spin out of her hands and clatter to the ground.

Wilbur ran to Grey. "You've got to wake up!" he hissed, slapping silver dust out of the were-weasel's fur. It was like trying to clean a shag carpet with bones.

Grey groaned and rolled over, rubbing his eyes.

". . . hurts . . ." he muttered.

"Harriet's in trouble!"

"I'm not in trouble!" yelled Harriet, ducking under another claw-slash. "I'm—just—err—temporarily disadvantaged—"

Grandmother whacked her alongside the head and sent her flying. Harriet crashed down heavily beside Grey.

Grey looked up groggily. "Sorry. The silver . . ."

"S'okay . . ." said Harriet, sounding a bit slurred herself from the blow to the head. "When the room stops spinning, I'll take care of it . . ."

Wilbur stood over Grey and Harriet. He had no weapons at all. Grandmother stalked toward him. Her nightgown had been shredded apart and she looked every inch the terrifying weasel-wolf.

If only he had a silver sword! Or a silver dagger, or even a silver paperweight! Something!

Harriet pushed herself up on her elbows. "Grey . . ." she said. "Grey, you gotta bite me . . ."

"Whuh . . . ?"

"Gotta . . . make me a were-weasel . . . so I can fight her . . ."

"Harriet, no!" said Wilbur.

"Can't let her eat you . . ." said Harriet. "Or put a collar on . . . Grey . . ." She got to her knees. "Careful. She's got a heckuva punch . . ."

Wilbur gulped. He couldn't let Harriet become a were-weasel, could he? Even if she really wanted to be one?

Grandmother lifted her clawed hands to strike.

GRANDMOTHER, *NO!*

# CHAPTER 20

"What?" said Grandmother.

"What?" said Harriet.

"What?" said Wilbur.

"Wha . . . ?" said Grey.

"Wrrfl?" said Snuffle.

Red threw her hood back and faced her grandmother. "Snuffle and I were talking. This isn't right."

("*How* were they talking?" whispered Harriet to Wilbur. Wilbur spread his hands helplessly and shook his head.)

"The weasel-wolves are scared of me," said Red. "Because I've been catching them. I thought they were animals, but Snuffle says they're people. I don't like having people scared of me. And people— hamster people—are scared of the weasel-wolves, and I bet they don't like it either."

"Wrrfl!" agreed Snuffle. He was clearly terrified of Grandmother, but he wasn't hiding anymore.

"And I've been hypnotizing the weasels for you," said Red, "but—but I don't want to do it anymore!"

She stamped her foot.

Harriet shook her head. "Never stamp your foot," she muttered. "We've been over this. Grey, come on!"

"Huh?" Grey tried to focus his eyes. "Wha' 'm I doin'?"

"Turning me into a were-weasel!"

"Harriet, no!" said Wilbur. "It'll be awful!"

"Red, dear," said Grandmother. "Can't we talk about this later?"

"No! Not when you're going to hurt Snuffle!" She stamped her foot again, perilously close to Harriet's fingers. Harriet yanked them out of the way.

"Gah!" Grandmother rolled her eyes. "I know this isn't your idea, Red. It's these awful lying weasel-wolves!"

"Snuffle didn't lie to me!"

"Wrrfl!"

"Come on, Grey . . ." Harriet held her arm in front of his face. "Come on! One bite!"

The were-hamster looked groggily at her arm. He opened his mouth in an enormous yawn and Harriet pushed forward.

"Don't you use the stare on me, young lady! I'm your grandmother! I'm . . . all . . . you've . . . got . . . all . . . you've . . ."

She took a step forward, then another, then slid to her knees.

ALL . . . YOU'VE . . . GOT . . . ZZZZZ . . .

The sounds of Grandmother's snores filled the clearing. But Grey was still groggy and confused. He tried to snap his teeth at Harriet, missed, and opened his mouth again.

Wilbur dove between them, knocking Harriet out of the way.

Grey's jaws closed . . . half an inch from Wilbur's hand. He looked blearily at the two hamsters. "Whrrrzzuh?"

"You are such a spoilsport, Wilbur," muttered Harriet. "I mean, I appreciate you trying to take a bite for me, but c'mon."

"If you still want to be a were-weasel when all of this is over, I won't stop you," said Wilbur. "But can we please get out of here first? *Before* you start shape-shifting all over the place?"

"Ugh. *Fine.* You sound like my mom."

Wilbur shook his head and sighed.

"Wrrfl," said Snuffle, and that seemed to say it all.

# CHAPTER 21

By the time Harriet, Mumfrey, Red, Snuffle, Shaggy Paw, Grey, and Grandmother all arrived back at the castle, even Harriet was getting tired.

Red and Snuffle had become fast friends over the course of the walk back.

"I still have no idea how they're talking to each other," whispered Wilbur.

Grey shrugged. "The very young have ways of communicating," he said.

"I am going to sleep for a week," announced Wilbur as the castle came into sight.

"Qwerk!" said Mumfrey, which was Quail for "You think you're tired!? I had to carry Grand-mother and Shaggy Paw the whole way!"

Shaggy Paw had eventually woken up, once Harriet pried the silver collar off him, but he was still wobbly from the cage. It had just been easier to load him up on Mumfrey.

Harriet wasn't looking forward to explaining the whole mess to her parents. Grown-ups could be very tiresome when you showed up with another adult hog-tied on top of a quail and often insisted on untying them before you could explain the situation.

She was a little surprised, therefore, to see that her father, the hamster king, was waiting for her outside the castle with a battalion of hamsters in armor.

"The laundry room?"

"She says that when the weasel-wolves eat her, it'll be easier to clean up that way."

Harriet sighed and began the princessly work of sorting it all out.

"You won't do anything bad to Grandmother, will you?" asked Red as the guards bundled the sleeping were-weasel into a wagon and drove her away.

"No," said Harriet. "I mean, she'll have to pay for her crimes. Kidnapping or . . . err . . . poaching . . . or illegal wildlife trafficking . . . I don't know. One of those. Some kind of crime. But after that, no."

I KNEW YOU WERE THE BEST, NICEST, SWEETEST PRINCESS IN THE WHOLE WIDE WORLD!

". . . let's not go nuts," said Harriet.

Red nodded. "I've decided I'm going to help the weasel-wolves," she said. "To make up for the bad stuff I did. Maybe if people knew that weasel-wolves mostly ate grasshoppers, they wouldn't be so scared of them."

"It might work," said Wilbur. "No more biting." He looked at Harriet. "And no more getting bitten . . ."

"I haven't given up," said Harriet. "I would make an awesome were-weasel." She turned to Grey. "What are you going to do?"

"Grandmother sold a lot of were-weasels before we stopped her," said Grey. "Somebody's got to find them." He rolled his shoulders. "Might as well be me."

"You could probably use some help," said Harriet. "Since once the moon's down, you'll need somebody to do the talking. The delicate negotiating. That stuff."

Wilbur thought of Harriet doing delicate negotiating. He shuddered. "I'll come too."

MIGHT BE USEFUL.

"Adventure doesn't sleep," said Harriet.

"Yes, but this hamster does!"

"Fiiiine . . ."

"I hate to mention this," said the hamster king, "but before you go anywhere, dear, there's still a whole pack of weasel-wolves sleeping in the stables. And your mother in the laundry room."

Harriet threw her hands in the air. "I don't know how this kingdom functions without me!"

"None of us do, dear," said the hamster king, putting an arm around her shoulders.

They went into the castle, arm in arm, to sort everything out and rest up for the next big adventure.

**THE END**

# SMOKING HOT BOOKS FROM VERNON!

★ "MOVE OVER, BABYMOUSE, THERE'S A NEW RODENT IN TOWN!"
— *SCHOOL LIBRARY JOURNAL*, STARRED REVIEW

★ "HARRIET IS HER OWN HAMSTER, BUT SHE TAKES HER PLACE PROUDLY ALONGSIDE BOTH DANNY DRAGONBREATH AND BABYMOUSE. CREATIVELY FRESH AND FEMINIST, WITH LAUGHS ON EVERY SINGLE PAGE."
— *KIRKUS REVIEWS*, STARRED REVIEW

★ "A BOOK WITH ALL THE MAKINGS OF A HIT. READERS WILL BE LAUGHING THEMSELVES SILLY."
— *PUBLISHERS WEEKLY*, STARRED REVIEW

★ "A JOY TO READ, AND WE CAN ONLY HOPE THAT HARRIET—LONG MAY SHE REIGN—WILL RETURN IN LATER INSTALLMENTS."
— *BOOKLIST*, STARRED REVIEW

# ABOUT THE AUTHOR

**Ursula Vernon** (www.ursulavernon.com) is an award-winning author and illustrator whose work has won two Hugo Awards and a Nebula Award, and been nominated for the World Fantasy Award and an Eisner. She loves birding, gardening, and spunky heroines. She is the first to admit that she would make a terrible princess.

# BONE IS A STAR!

★ "AS HILARIOUS AS IT IS FUN. MAKE ROOM ON THE SHELVES FOR THIS NOT SO FRILLY PRINCESS."
—*SCHOOL LIBRARY JOURNAL,* STARRED REVIEW

"HARRIET IS AS DELIGHTFUL AS EVER. . . . AS LONG AS VERNON KEEPS HARRIET'S ADVENTURES COMING, FANS NEW AND OLD ARE BOUND TO KEEP READING THEM." —*BOOKLIST*

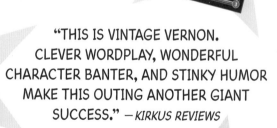

"THIS IS VINTAGE VERNON. CLEVER WORDPLAY, WONDERFUL CHARACTER BANTER, AND STINKY HUMOR MAKE THIS OUTING ANOTHER GIANT SUCCESS." —*KIRKUS REVIEWS*

★ "READERS WILL HAVE A BALL WITH THIS HILARIOUS, CHARMING STORY."
—*KIRKUS REVIEWS,* STARRED REVIEW